There is a treasure that delights and enriches beyond gold or silver: the treasure of a great story. Candlewick Treasures are exquisite editions of some of the world's greatest stories — both well-loved favorites and little-known gems — each illustrated by one of today's finest picture book artists.

A pleasure not only to read, but also to hold, these are classic works of literature to collect and keep forever.

❖

Elsie Piddock
Skips in Her
Sleep

ELEANOR FARJEON

illustrated by
CHARLOTTE VOAKE

CANDLEWICK PRESS
CAMBRIDGE, MASSACHUSETTS

Eleanor Farjeon (1881–1965) was one of the most important children's writers of the twentieth century. A fine poet, she also wrote many stories for the young. She had no formal education and spent her childhood reading in her father's library or playing imaginative games with her brother Harry. Her writing was a natural extension of this, its immediacy and energy the product of "a life kept always young."
Elsie Piddock Skips in Her Sleep, a particular favorite of the author and widely regarded as a miniature masterpiece, is taken from her second collection of stories, *Martin Pippin in the Daisy Field* (1937). In 1956 her achievements were acknowledged with the award of both the Carnegie Medal and the Hans Christian Andersen International Medal. In her honor, a prize bearing her name is now awarded annually to mark an outstanding contribution to children's literature.

Charlotte Voake was singled out
by Eleanor Farjeon's nephew, Gervase,
as the ideal artist to interpret *Elsie
Piddock Skips in Her Sleep*. Her illustrations display a natural exuberance and
lightness of touch that characterize
Farjeon's own work. A much admired
artist, Charlotte Voake has
been honored for
her illustrations
with a Parents'
Choice Award
and has been
shortlisted four
times for the
prestigious Kurt
Maschler Award in Britain.
Her other Candlewick Press titles include
the acclaimed nursery anthologies *Over
the Moon* and *The Three Little Pigs and
Other Favorite Nursery Stories*, as well as
her own stories *Mr. Davies and the Baby,
Ginger*, and *Mrs. Goose's Baby*. She is
married and has two children.

Elsie Piddock lived in
Glynde under Caburn, where
lots of other little girls lived too.
They lived mostly on bread-and-
butter, because their mothers were
too poor to buy cake. As soon
as Elsie began to hear, she heard
the other little girls skipping
every evening after school in the
lane outside her mother's cottage.
Swish-swish! went the rope
through the air. Tappity-tap! went
the little girls' feet on the ground.

Mumble-umble-umble! went the children's voices, saying a rhyme that the skipper could skip to. In course of time, Elsie not only heard the sounds, but understood what they were all about, and then the mumble-umble turned itself into words like this:

"ANdy SPANdy SUGARdy CANdy,

FRENCH ALmond ROCK!

Breadandbutterforyoursupper's-

allyourmother's-

GOT!"

The second bit went twice as fast as the first bit, and when the little girls said it Elsie Piddock, munching her supper, always munched her mouthful of bread-and-butter in

double-quick time. She wished
she had some Sugardy-Candy-
French-Almond-Rock to suck during
the first bit, but she never had.

When Elsie Piddock was three
years old, she asked her mother for
a skipping-rope.

"You're too little," said her mother.
"Bide a bit till you're a bigger girl,
then you shall have one."

Elsie pouted and said no more.
But in the middle of the night her
parents were wakened by something
going Slap-slap! on the
floor, and there was
Elsie in her
night-gown
skipping with
her father's
braces.

She skipped till her feet caught in the tail of them, and she tumbled down and cried. But she had skipped ten times running first.

"Bless my buttons, mother!" said Mr. Piddock. "The child's a born skipper."

And Mrs. Piddock jumped out of bed full of pride, rubbed Elsie's elbows for her, and said: "There-a-there now! Dry your tears, and tomorrow you shall have a skip-rope all of your own."

So Elsie dried her eyes on the hem of her night-gown; and in the morning, before he went to work, Mr. Piddock got a little cord, just the right length, and made two little wooden handles to go on the ends.

With this Elsie skipped all day,
scarcely stopping to eat her
breakfast of bread-and-butter, and
her dinner of butter-and-bread.
And in the evening, when the
schoolchildren were gathered in
the lane, Elsie went out among
them, and began to skip with
the best.

"Oh!" cried Joan Challon, who was the champion skipper of them all, "just look at little Elsie Piddock skipping as never so!"

All the skippers stopped to look, and then to wonder. Elsie Piddock certainly *did* skip as never so, and they called to their mothers to come and see. And the mothers in the lane came  to their doors, and threw up their hands, and cried: "Little Elsie Piddock is a born skipper!"

By the time she was five she could outskip any of them: whether in

"Andy Spandy," "Lady, Lady, drop your Purse," "Charley Parley stole some Barley," or whichever of the games it might be.

By the time she was six her name and fame were known to all the villages in the county. And by the time she was seven, the fairies heard of her. They were fond of

skipping themselves, and they had a special Skipping-Master who taught them new skips every month at the new moon. As they skipped they chanted:

"The High Skip,

The Sly Skip,

The Skip Like a Feather,

The Long Skip,

The Strong Skip,

And the Skip All Together!

The Slow Skip,

The Toe Skip,

The Skip Double-Double,

The Fast Skip,

The Last Skip,

And the Skip

Against Trouble!"

All these skips had their own
meanings, and were made up by
the Skipping-Master, whose name
was Andy-Spandy. He was very
proud of his fairies, because they
skipped better than the fairies of
any other county; but he was also
very severe with them if they did
not please him.

One night he scolded Fairy Heels-
o'-Lead for skipping badly, and
praised Fairy Flea-Foot for skipping
well. Then Fairy Heels-o'-Lead
sniffed and snuffed, and said:

"Hhm-hhm-hhm! there's a little girl in Glynde who could skip Flea-Foot round the moon and back again. A born skipper she is, and she skips as never so."

"What is her name?" asked Andy-Spandy.

"Her name is Elsie Piddock, and she has skipped down every village far and near, from Didling to Wannock."

"Go and fetch her here!" commanded Andy-Spandy.

Off went Heels-o'-Lead, and poked her head through Elsie's little window under the eaves, crying: "Elsie Piddock! Elsie Piddock! there's a Skipping-Match

16

on Caburn, and Fairy Flea-Foot says she can skip better than you."

Elsie Piddock was fast asleep, but the words got into her dream, so she hopped out of bed with her eyes closed, took her skipping-rope, and followed Heels-o'-Lead to the top of Mount Caburn, where Andy-Spandy and the fairies were waiting for them.

"Skip, Elsie Piddock!"
said Andy-Spandy,
"and show us what
you're worth!"

Elsie twirled
her rope and skipped
in her sleep, and as she skipped
she murmured:

"ANdy SPANdy SUGARdy CANdy,

FRENCH ALmond ROCK!

Breadandbutterforyoursupper's-

allyourmother's-

GOT!"

Andy-Spandy watched her
skipping with his eyes as sharp as
needles, but he could find no fault
with it, nor could the fairies.

"Very good, as far as it goes!" said Andy-Spandy. "Now let us see how far it *does* go. Stand forth, Elsie and Flea-Foot, for the Long Skip."

Elsie had never done the Long Skip, and if she had had all her wits about her she wouldn't have known what Andy-Spandy meant; but as she was dreaming, she understood him perfectly. So she twirled her rope, and as it came over jumped as far along the ground as she could, about twelve feet from where she had started. Then Flea-Foot did the Long Skip, and skipped clean out of sight.

"Hum!" said Andy-Spandy. "Now, Elsie Piddock, let us see you do the Strong Skip."

Once more Elsie understood what

was wanted of her; she put both feet together, jumped her rope, and came down with all her strength, so that her heels sank into the ground. Then Flea-Foot did the Strong Skip, and sank into the ground as deep as her waist.

"Hum!" said Andy-Spandy. "And now, Elsie Piddock, let us see you do the Skip All Together."

At his words, all the fairies leaped to their ropes, and began skipping as lively as they could, and Elsie with them. An hour went by, two hours, and three hours; one by one the fairies fell down exhausted, and Elsie Piddock skipped on. Just before morning she was skipping all by herself.

Then Andy-Spandy wagged his head and said: "Elsie Piddock, you are a born skipper. There's no tiring you at all.

And for that you shall come once a month to Caburn when the moon is new, and I will teach you to skip till a year is up. And after that I'll wager there won't be mortal or fairy to touch you."

Andy-Spandy was as good as his word. Twelve times during the next year Elsie Piddock rose up in her sleep with the new moon, and went to the top of Mount Caburn. There she took her place among the fairies, and learned to do all the tricks of the skipping-rope, until she did them better than any. At the end of the year she did the High Skip so well, that she skipped right over the moon.

In the Sly Skip not a fairy could catch her, or know where she would skip to next; so artful was she, that she could skip through the lattice of a skeleton leaf, and never break it.

She redoubled the Skip Double-Double, in which you only had to double yourself up twice round the skipping-rope before it came down. Elsie Piddock did it four times.

In the Fast Skip, she skipped so fast that you couldn't see her, though she stood on the same spot all the time.

In the Last Skip, when all the fairies skipped over the same rope in turn, running round and round till they made a mistake from giddiness, Elsie never got giddy, and never made a mistake, and was always left in last.

In the Slow Skip, she skipped
so slow that a mole had time to
throw up his hill under her rope
before she came down.

In the Toe Skip, when all the
others skipped on their tip-toes,
Elsie never touched a grass-blade
with more than the edge of her
toe-nail.

In the Skip Against Trouble,
she skipped so joyously that
Andy-Spandy himself chuckled
with delight.

In the Long Skip she skipped
from Caburn to the other end of
Sussex, and had to be fetched
back by the wind.

In the Strong Skip, she went right
under the earth, as a diver goes
under the sea, and the rabbits,

whose burrows she had disturbed, handed her up again.

But in the Skip Like a Feather she came down like gossamer, so that she could alight on a spider-thread and never shake the dew-drop off.

And in the Skip All Together, she could skip down the whole tribe of fairies, and remain as fresh as a daisy. Nobody had ever found out how long Elsie Piddock could skip without getting tired, for everybody else got tired first. Even Andy-Spandy didn't know.

At the end of the year he said to her: "Elsie Piddock, I have taught you all. Bring me your skipping-rope, and you shall have a prize."

Elsie gave her rope to Andy-Spandy, and he licked the two little wooden handles, first the one and then the other. When he handed the rope back to her, one of the handles was made of Sugar Candy, and the other of French Almond Rock.

"There!" said Andy-Spandy. "Though you suck them never so, they will never grow less, and you shall therefore suck sweet all your life. And as long as you are little enough to skip with this rope, you shall skip as I have taught you. But when you are too big for this rope, and must get a new one, you will no longer be able to do all the fairy skips that you have learned, although you will still skip better in the mortal way than any other girl that ever was born. Good-bye, Elsie Piddock."

"Aren't I ever going to skip for you again?" asked Elsie Piddock in her sleep.

But Andy-Spandy didn't answer. For morning had come over the Downs, and the fairies disappeared, and Elsie Piddock went back to bed.

If Elsie had been famous for her skipping before this fairy year, you can imagine what she became after it. She created so much wonder, that she hardly dared to show all she could do.

Nevertheless, for another year she did such incredible things, that people came from far and near to see her skip over the church spire, or through the split oak-tree in the Lord's Park, or across the river at its widest point.

When there was trouble in her
mother's house, or in any house
in the village, Elsie Piddock
skipped so gaily that the
trouble was forgotten
in laughter.
And when
she skipped
all the old
games in
Glynde, along
with the little
girls, and they sang:

"ANdy SPANdy SUGARdy CANdy,

FRENCH ALmond ROCK!

Breadandbutterforyoursupper's-

allyourmother's-

GOT!"

Elsie Piddock said: "It
aren't all *I've* got!" and gave
them a suck of her skipping-rope
handles all round. And on the
night of the new moon, she always
led the children up Mount Caburn,
where she skipped more marvel-
lously than ever. In fact, it was Elsie
Piddock who established the custom

29

of New-Moon-Skipping on Caburn.

But at the end of another year she had grown too big to skip with her little rope. She laid it away in a box, and went on skipping with a longer one. She still skipped as never so, but her fairy tricks were laid by with the rope, and though her friends teased her to do the marvellous things she used to do, Elsie Piddock only laughed, and shook her head, and never told why. In time, when she was still the pride and wonder of her village, people would say: "Ah, but you should ha' seen her when she was a littling! Why, she could skip through her mother's keyhole!" And in more time, these stories became a legend that nobody believed. And in still more time, Elsie grew up (though never very much), and became a little woman, and gave up skipping, because skipping-time was over. After fifty years or so, nobody remembered that she had ever skipped at all. Only Elsie knew. For when times were hard, and they often were, she sat by the hearth with her dry crust and no butter, and sucked the Sugar Candy that Andy-Spandy had given her for life.

IT WAS EVER and ever so long
afterwards. Three new Lords had
walked in the Park since the day
when Elsie Piddock had skipped
through the split oak. Changes had
come in the village; old families
had died out, new families had
arrived; others had moved away to
distant parts, the Piddocks among
them. Farms had changed hands,
cottages had been pulled down,
and new ones had been built. But
Mount Caburn was as it always had
been, and as the people came to

think it always would be. And still
the children kept the custom of
going there each new moon to skip.
Nobody remembered how this custom had come about, it was too far
back in the years. But customs are
customs, and the child who could
not skip the new moon in on
Caburn stayed at home and cried.

Then a new Lord came to the
Park; one not born a Lord, who had
grown rich in trade, and bought the
old estate. Soon after his coming,
changes began to take place more
violent than the pulling down of
cottages. The new Lord began to
shut up footpaths and destroy
rights of way. He stole the
Common rights here and there,
as he could. In his greed for more

than he had got, he raised rents
and pressed the people harder than
they could bear. But bad as the
high rents were to them, they did
not mind these so much as the loss
of their old rights. They fought the
new Lord, trying to keep what
had been theirs for centuries, and
sometimes they won the fight,
but oftener lost it. The constant
quarrels bred a spirit of anger
between them and the Lord, and
out of hate he was prepared to do
whatever he could to spite them.

Amongst the lands over which
he exercised a certain power was
Caburn. This had been always
open to the people, and the Lord
determined if he could to close it.
Looking up the old deeds, he

discovered that, though the Down was his, he was obliged to leave a way upon it by which the people could go from one village to another. For hundreds of years they had made a short cut of it over the top.

The Lord's Lawyer told him that, by the wording of the deeds, he could never stop the people from travelling by way of the Downs.

"Can't I!" snorted the Lord. "Then at least I will make them travel a long way round!"

And he had plans drawn up to enclose the whole of the top of Caburn, so that nobody could walk on it. This meant that the people must trudge miles round the base, as they passed from place to place. The Lord gave out that he needed

Mount Caburn to build great
factories on.

The village was up in arms to
defend its rights.

"Can he do it?" they asked those
who knew; and they were told:
"It is not quite certain, but we fear
he can." The Lord himself was not
quite certain either but he went
on with his plans, and each new
move was watched with anger and
anxiety by the villagers. And not
only by the villagers; for the fairies
saw that their own skipping-
ground was threatened. How could
they ever skip there again when
the grass was turned to cinders,
and the new moon blackened by
chimney-smoke?

The Lawyer said to the Lord: "The

people will fight you tooth and nail."

"Let 'em!" blustered the Lord; and he asked uneasily: "Have they a leg to stand on?"

"Just half a leg," said the Lawyer. "It would be as well not to begin building yet, and if you can come to terms with them you'd better."

The Lord sent word to the villagers that, though he undoubtedly could do what he pleased, he would, out of his good heart, restore to them a footpath he had blocked, if they would give up all pretensions to Caburn.

"Footpath, indeed!" cried stout John Maltman, among his cronies at the Inn. "What's a footpath to Caburn? Why, our mothers skipped there as children, and our children skip there now. And we hope to see our children's children skip there. If Caburn top be built over, 'twill fair break my little Ellen's heart."

"Ay, and my Margery's," said another.

"And my Mary's and Kitty's!" cried a third. Others spoke up, for nearly all had daughters whose joy it was to skip on Caburn at the new moon.

John Maltman turned to their best adviser, who had studied the matter closely, and asked: "What think ye? Have we a leg to stand on?"

"Only half a one," said the other. "I doubt if you can stop him. It might be as well to come to terms."

"None of his footpaths for us," swore stout John Maltman. "We'll fight the matter out."

So things were left for a little, and

each side wondered what the next
move would be. Only the people
knew in their hearts that they must
be beaten in the end and the Lord
was sure of his victory. So sure, that
he had great loads of bricks ordered;
but he did not begin building for
fear the people might grow violent,
and perhaps burn his ricks and
destroy his property. The only thing
he did was to put a wire fence round
the top of Caburn, and set a keeper
there to send the people round it.

The people broke the fence in
many places, and jumped it,
and crawled under it;

and as the keeper could not be everywhere at once, many of them crossed the Down almost under his nose.

One evening, just before the new moon was due, Ellen Maltman went into the woods to cry. For she was the best skipper under Mount Caburn, and the thought that she would never skip there again made her more unhappy than she had ever thought she could be. While she was crying in the dark, she felt a hand on her shoulder, and a voice said to her: "Crying for trouble, my dear? That'll never do!"

The voice might have been the voice of a withered leaf, it was so light and dry; but it was also kind, so Ellen checked her sobs and said:

"It's a big trouble, ma'am, there's no remedy against it *but* to cry."

"Why, yes, there is," said the withered voice. "Ye should skip against trouble, my dear."

At this Ellen's sobs burst forth anew. "I'll never skip no more!" she wailed. "If I can't skip the new moon in on Caburn, I'll never skip no more."

"And why can't you skip the new moon in on Caburn?" asked the voice.

Then Ellen told her.

After a little pause the voice spoke quietly out of the darkness.
"It's more than you will break their hearts if they cannot skip on Caburn. And it must not be, it must not be. Tell me your name."

"Ellen Maltman, ma'am, and I do love skipping. I can skip down anybody, ma'am, and they say I skip as never so!"

"They do, do they?" said the withered voice. "Well, Ellen, run you home and tell them this. They are to go to this Lord and tell him he shall have his way and build on Caburn, if he will first take down the fence and let all who have ever skipped there skip there once more by turns, at the new moon. *All*, mind you, Ellen. And when the last skipper skips the last skip, he may lay his first brick. And let it be written out on paper, and signed and sealed."

"But ma'am!" said Ellen, wondering.

"No words, child. Do as I tell you."

And the withered voice sounded so
compelling that Ellen resisted no
more. She ran straight to the village,
and told her story to everybody.

At first they could hardly swallow
it; and even when they had
swallowed it, they said: "But what's
the sense of it?" But Ellen persisted
and persisted; something of the
spirit of the old voice got into her
words, and against their reason the
people began to think it was the
thing to do. To cut a long story
short they sent the message
to the Lord next day.

The Lord could scarcely believe
his ears. He rubbed his hands,
and chortled at the
people for fools.

"They've come to terms!" he
sneered. "I shall have the Down,
and keep my footpath too. Well,
they shall have their Skipping-
Party; and the moment it is
ended, up go my factories!"

The paper was drawn
out, signed by both
parties in the presence
of witnesses, and duly
sealed; and on the night of the new
moon, the Lord invited a party of
his friends to go with him to Caburn
to see the sight.

And what a sight it was for them
to see; every little girl in the village
was there with her skipping-rope,
from the toddlers to those who had
just turned up their hair. Nay, even
the grown maidens and the young

mothers were there; and the very
matrons too had come with ropes.
Had not they once as children
skipped on Caburn? And the message
had said "All." Yes, and others were
there, others they could not see:

Andy-Spandy and his fairy team,
Heels-o'-Lead, Flea-Foot, and all
of the rest, were gathered round to
watch with bright fierce eyes
the last great skipping on their
precious ground.

The skipping began. The toddlers first, a skip or so apiece, a stumble, and they fell out. The Lord and his party laughed aloud at the comical mites, and at another time the villagers would have laughed too. But there was no laughter in them tonight. Their eyes were bright and fierce like those of the fairies. After the toddlers the little girls skipped in the order of their ages, and as they got older, the skipping got better. In the thick of the school-children, "This will take some time," said the Lord impatiently. And when Ellen Maltman's turn came, and she went into her thousands, he grew restive. But even she, who could skip as never so, tired at last; her foot tripped, and she fell on the ground with a little sob. None lasted even half her time; of those who followed some were better, some were worse, than others; and in the small hours the older women were beginning to take their turn. Few of them kept it up for half a minute; they hopped and puffed bravely, but their skipping days were done. As they had laughed at the babies, so now the Lord's friends jibed at the babies' grandmothers.

"Soon over now," said the Lord, as the oldest of the women who had come to skip, a fat old dame of sixty-seven, stepped out and twirled her rope. Her foot caught in it; she staggered, dropped the rope, and hid her face in her hands.

"Done!" shouted the Lord; and he brandished at the crowd a trowel and a brick which he had brought with him. "Clear out, the lot of you! I am going to lay the first brick. The skipping's ended!"

"No, if you please," said a gentle withered voice, "it is my turn now." And out of the crowd stepped a tiny tiny woman, so very old, so very bent and fragile, that she seemed to be no bigger than a little child.

"You!" cried the Lord. "Who
are *you*?"

"My name is Elsie Piddock, if
you please, and I am a hundred
and nine years old. For the last
seventy-nine years I have lived over
the border, but I was born in

Glynde, and I skipped on Caburn as a child." She spoke like one in a dream, and her eyes were closed.

"Elsie Piddock! Elsie Piddock!" the name ran in a whisper round the crowd.

"Elsie Piddock!" murmured Ellen Maltman. "Why, Mum, I thought Elsie Piddock was just a tale."

"Nay, Elsie Piddock was no tale!" said the fat woman who had skipped last. "My mother Joan skipped with her many a time, and told me tales you never would believe."

"Elsie Piddock!" they all breathed again; and a wind seemed to fly round Mount Caburn, shrilling the name with glee. But it was no wind, it was Andy-Spandy and his fairy team, for they had seen the skipping-

rope in the tiny woman's hands.
One of the handles was made of
Sugar Candy, and the other was
made of French Almond Rock.

But the new Lord had never even
heard of Elsie Piddock as a story; so
laughing coarsely once again, he
said: "One more bump for an old
woman's bones! Skip, Elsie Piddock,
and show us what you're worth."

"Yes, skip, Elsie Piddock," cried
Andy-Spandy and the fairies, "and
show them what you're worth!"

Then Elsie Piddock stepped into
the middle of the onlookers, twirled
her baby rope over her
little shrunken body,
and began to skip.
And she skipped
as NEVER so!

First of all she skipped:

"ANdy SPANdy SUGARdy CANdy,
FRENCH ALmond ROCK!
Breadandbutterforyoursupper's-
allyourmother's-
GOT!"

And nobody could find fault with
her skipping. Even the Lord gasped:
"Wonderful! wonderful for an old
woman!" But Ellen Maltman, who
knew, whispered: "Oh, Mum! 'tis
wonderful for *any*body! And oh,
Mum, do but see—she's skipping
in her sleep!"

It was true. Elsie Piddock, shrunk
to the size of seven years old, was
sound asleep, skipping the new

moon in with her baby rope that
was up to all the tricks. An hour
went by, two hours, three
hours. There was no stopping her,
and no tiring her. The people
gasped, the Lord fumed, and the
fairies turned head-over-heels
for joy. When morning broke the
Lord cried: "That's enough!"

But Elsie Piddock went on
skipping.

"Time's up!" cried the Lord.

"When I skip my last skip, you
shall lay your first brick," said Elsie
Piddock.

The villagers broke into a cheer.

"Signed and sealed, my Lord,
signed and sealed," said Elsie
Piddock.

"But hang it, old woman, you

can't go on for ever!" cried
the Lord.

"Oh yes, I can," said
Elsie Piddock. And
on she went.

At midday the
Lord shouted: "Will
the woman never stop?"

"No, she won't," said Elsie
Piddock. And she didn't.

"Then I'll stop you!" stormed the
Lord, and made a grab at her.

"Now for a Sly Skip," said Elsie
Piddock, and skipped right
through his thumb and forefinger.

"Hold her, you!" yelled the Lord
to his Lawyer.

"Now for a High Skip," said Elsie
Piddock, and as the Lawyer darted
at her, she skipped right over the

highest lark singing in the sun.

The villagers shouted for glee,
and the Lord and his friends
were furious. Forgotten was the
compact signed and sealed—their
one thought now was to seize the
maddening old woman, and stop
her skipping by sheer force.

But they couldn't. She played all
her tricks on them: High Skip,
Slow Skip, Sly Skip, Toe Skip,

Long Skip, Fast Skip, Strong Skip, but never Last Skip. On and on and on she went. When the sun began to set, she was still skipping.

"Can we never rid the Down of the old thing?" cried the Lord desperately.

"No," answered Elsie Piddock in her sleep, "the Down will never be rid of me more. It's the children of Glynde I'm skipping for, to hold the Down for them and theirs for ever; it's Andy-Spandy I'm skipping for once again, for through him I've sucked sweet all my life. Oh, Andy, even you never knew how long Elsie Piddock could go on skipping!"

"The woman's mad!" cried the Lord. "Signed and sealed doesn't hold with a madwoman. Skip or no skip, I shall lay the first brick!"

He plunged his trowel into the ground, and forced his brick down into the hole as a token of his possession of the land.

"Now," said Elsie Piddock, "for a Strong Skip!"

Right on the top of the brick she skipped, and down underground she sank out of sight, bearing the brick beneath her. Wild with rage, the Lord dived after her. Up came Elsie Piddock skipping blither than ever—but the Lord never came up again. The Lawyer ran to look down the hole; but there was no sign of him. The Lawyer reached his arm down the hole; but there was no reaching him. The Lawyer dropped a pebble down the hole; and no one heard it fall. So strong had Elsie Piddock skipped the Strong Skip.

The Lawyer shrugged his shoulders, and he and the Lord's friends left Mount Caburn for good and all. Oh, how joyously Elsie Piddock skipped then!

"Skip Against Trouble!" cried she, and skipped so that everyone present burst into happy laughter. To the tune of it she skipped the Long Skip, clean out of sight. And the people went home to tea. Caburn was saved for their children, and for the fairies, for ever.

But that wasn't the end of Elsie Piddock; she has never stopped skipping on Caburn since, for Signed and Sealed is Signed and

Sealed. Not many have seen her,
because she knows all the tricks;
but if you go to Caburn at the new
moon, you may catch a glimpse
of a tiny bent figure, no bigger than
a child, skipping all by itself in its
sleep, and hear a gay little voice,
like the voice of a dancing
yellow leaf, singing:

"ANdy SPANdy SUGARdy CANdy,

FRENCH ALmond ROCK!

Breadandbutterforyoursupper's-

allyourmother's-

GOT!"

For
Eileen Colwell, storyteller,
because Eleanor Farjeon thought her
"just right for Elsie Piddock"

Other Candlewick Treasures:

The Canterville Ghost
Little Long-nose · *The Lord Fish*
Rikki-tikki-tavi · *A White Heron*

Text copyright © 1937, 1997 by Gervase Farjeon
Illustrations copyright © 1997 by Charlotte Voake

All rights reserved.

First U.S. edition 1997

Library of Congress Cataloging-in-Publication Data

Farjeon, Eleanor.
Elsie Piddock skips in her sleep / Eleanor Farjeon ;
illustrated by Charlotte Voake. — 1st U.S. ed.
(Candlewick treasures) Summary: Celebrated since childhood for how
well she skips rope, 109-year-old Elsie Piddock once again skips
to save her English country town.
ISBN 0-7636-0133-0
[1. Rope skipping—Fiction. 2. England—Fiction.]
I. Voake, Charlotte, ill. II. Title. III. Series.
PZ7.F229E1 1997 [Fic]—dc20   96-26250

2 4 6 8 10 9 7 5 3 1

Printed in Italy

This book was typeset in Calligraphic Bold.
The pictures were done in pen and ink and watercolor.

Candlewick Press
2067 Massachusetts Avenue
Cambridge, Massachusetts 02140